About the Bank Street Ready-to-Read Series

More than seventy-five years of educational research, innovative teaching, and quality publishing have earned The Bank Street College of Education its reputation as America's most trusted name in early childhood education.

Because no two children are exactly alike in their development, the Bank Street Ready-to-Read series is written on three levels to accommodate the individual stages of reading readiness of children ages three through eight.

○ ***Level 1:*** **Getting Ready to Read (Pre-K–Grade 1)**
Level 1 books are perfect for reading aloud with children who are getting ready to read or just starting to read words or phrases. These books feature large type, repetition, and simple sentences.

● ***Level 2:*** **Reading Together (Grades 1–3)**
These books have slightly smaller type and longer sentences. They are ideal for children beginning to read by themselves who may need help.

○ ***Level 3:*** **I Can Read It Myself (Grades 2–3)**
These stories are just right for children who can read independently. They offer more complex and challenging stories and sentences.

All three levels of The Bank Street Ready-to-Read books make it easy to select the books most appropriate for your child's development and enable him or her to grow with the series step by step. The levels purposely overlap to reinforce skills and further encourage reading.

We feel that making reading fun is the single most important thing anyone can do to help children become good readers. We hope you will become part of Bank Street's long tradition of learning through sharing.

The Bank Street College of Education

To Julie and Karen
— B.B.

For Cody and Cooper
and the Two Hill Kids
— R.O.

For a free color catalog describing Gareth Stevens' list of high-quality books and multimedia programs, call 1-800-542-2595 (USA) or 1-800-461-9120 (Canada). Gareth Stevens Publishing's Fax: (414) 225-0377.

Library of Congress Cataloging-in-Publication Data

Boegehold, Betty Doyle.
The fight / by Betty D. Boegehold; illustrated by Robin Oz.
p. cm. -- (Bank Street ready-to-read)
Summary: An accidental bump starts a gigantic fight in the schoolyard when the students forget to use their heads and use their fists instead.
ISBN 0-8368-2420-2 (lib. bdg.)
[1. Schools--Fiction. 2. Behavior--Fiction. 3. Stories in rhyme.]
I. Oz, Robin, ill. II. Title. III. Series.
PZ8.3.B59954Fi 1999
[E]--dc21 99-18572

This edition first published in 1999 by
Gareth Stevens Publishing
1555 North RiverCenter Drive, Suite 201
Milwaukee, Wisconsin 53212 USA

Printed in Mexico

1 2 3 4 5 6 7 8 9 03 02 01 00 99

Bank Street Ready-to-Read™

The Fight

by Betty D. Boegehold
Illustrated by Robin Oz

A Byron Preiss Book

Gareth Stevens Publishing
MILWAUKEE

What do you think happened
in the schoolyard?

This is Dan
who bumped into Fran,
which started the fight
in the schoolyard.

This is Will
being pushed by Fran,
who was bumped by Dan,
which started the fight
in the schoolyard.

This is Phil
being punched by Will,
who was pushed by Fran,
who was bumped by Dan,
which started the fight
in the schoolyard.

This is Lil
who was hit by Phil,
who he thought was Will,
who was pushed by Fran,
who was bumped by Dan,
which started the fight
in the schoolyard.

This is the teacher
named Mr. Hart,
who rushed to pull
the kids apart
and stop the fight
in the schoolyard.

This is the stone
sticking out of the ground
that tripped Mr. Hart
and spun him around.

Then Mr. Hart fell
into a swing.
The swing took off
like a living thing!

It gave Mr. Hart
the bumpiest ride,
before it dumped him
onto the slide!
Down, down, down
he went until—

he landed on top of Lil and Phil,
who then crashed into little Will.

This is the mound
that rose from the ground
with Lil and Phil,
as well as Will,
and Fran and Dan,
and Mr. Hart,
all in a pile
in the schoolyard.

This is the nurse
who heard the fuss.
This is the driver
who stopped his bus.

This is the crowd
that came on the run
to stop the fight
in the schoolyard.

These are the kids
they pulled apart,
and there they found
poor Mr. Hart
flat on the ground
in the schoolyard.

"How did it start?"
asked Mr. Hart.

"It was Will!" said Phil.
"It was Phil!" cried Lil.
"It was Dan!" shouted Fran.
"It was dumb!" groaned Dan.
And then he said,
"I used my fists
and not my head!"

Phil said, "You're right.
This is a mess.
To top it off
we missed recess!"

One by one,
they did admit
they'd bumped and pushed
and punched and hit
until they forgot
what started it—

FIRST AID

that silly fight in the schoolyard!